Clint Faraday Mysteries
#11
See You In Hell

Rednecks threatening the Indios on the comarca?
Not while Clint Faraday is alive and kicking!
But what the hell was it really about?

Clint Faraday Mysteries
#11
See You In Hell

Contents

An Incident   pg. 1
A Dead Redneck   pg. 8
What Cargo?   pg. 18
A Clue or Two   pg. 26
50-50   pg. 35
Why Here?   pg. 40
Another Player   pg. 46
Coming Together   pg. 53
The Wait   pg. 62
Calls and Conversations pg. 68

About the author

CD was born in Lakeland, Florida. His education is in genetics and botany. He has traveled over much of the world, particularly when he was in music as a rock rhythm guitarist with some well-known bands in the late sixties and early seventies. He has worked as a high steel worker and as a longshoreman, clerk, orchidist, bar owner, salvage yard manager and landscaper – among other things.

CD began writing fiction in 1984 and has more than 115 books published as of this time in SciFi, murder, orchid culture and various other fields.

He now resides in Bocas del Toro and David, Panamá, where he continues research into epiphytic plants. He loves the culture of the indigenous people and counts a majority of his closer friends among that group. Several have "adopted" him as their father. He funds those he can afford through the universities where they have all excelled. "The Indios are very intelligent people, they are simply too poor (in material things and money. Culturally, they are very wealthy) to pursue higher education."

CD loves Panamá and the people. He plans to spend the rest of his life in the paradise that is Panamá

- Estrelita Suarez V.

CD is involved in research of natural cancer cure at this time. It has proven effective in all cases, so far. It is based on a plant that has been in use for thousands of years, is safe, available, and cheap. He has studied botany, and was cured of a serious lymphoma with use of the plant, *Ambrosia peruviana*.

Information about this cure is free on the FaceBook page, Ambrosia peruviana for cancer. CD asks only that all who try it please report on its effectiveness on that group.

See You In Hell

<u>*An Incident*</u>

Clint Faraday, retired PI from Florida, USA, stepped off the Changuinola, Bocas del Toro, Panamá bus at the Rambala road on the twelfth. He was visiting friends in Miramar earlier, and was heading to David when he got a call from Ernesto, an Indio friend, who said there was about to be big trouble on the comarca. Some gringos were there, treating the people like dirt. They were armed and Orlando, the chief, didn't want to call the Policia Nacional onto the comarca. Clint said he was close and would meet Ernesto at the Rambala road. He slipped his Glock into the holster and waited less than three minutes for Ernesto to come in his old Jeep. He didn't say much as they rode the distance onto the rough road into the comarca. Ernesto told him the gringos seemed to think they had the right to go anywhere and treated the natives like servants. They were drinking beer, but huge amounts of it. They were driving one of the very few Hummers ever seen in the area.

Clint came into the picturesque little village and immediately saw the Hummer sitting outside the tienda, with a number of the Indios milling around. He went inside to find four large and slightly obese men threatening the woman who ran the place with a rifle. Clint took his Glock from the holster and shoved the muzzle roughly into the ear of the one with the rifle and said "Drop it or I drop you! Now!"

He dropped it. Clint stepped back and told Ernesto to collect all the guns, knives, or baseball bats – any weapons – these clowns were carrying. Ernesto waved to the several Indio men in front and picked up the rifle. One of the other gringos started to reach for a pistol he was wearing and Clint aimed directly between his eyes and said, "Give it a go, turkey! I'll have a turkey shoot!"

He told the Indios to collect every weapon of *any* type these were carrying.

"They ain't got no permission to get in my car!" one of them spat. "They got to get a warrant to get in my car!"

"No. They don't," Clint replied easily. "This is the comarca."

"So the fuck what?" he demanded.

"The comarca has its own laws. Laws from anywhere else don't apply. One of those laws is that nobody carries a weapon or even brings it onto the comarca." He was making it up, but that was probably what the laws of the comarca were. Clint knew and loved the people.

Orlando drove up in his old Toyota truck and came inside, where Ernesto told him what was happening while the rednecks were arguing with Clint. The several Indios were going through the Hummer carefully and had three more rifles, two pistols, a lot of hunting knives and so forth, and some assorted things they laid out because they didn't know what they were.

"You will produce permits to have these things here in Panamá," Orlando said sternly. "There are no permits for weapons on the comarca. These things will be confiscated."

"Hey! Who ... what is he saying? I ain't got much EE-spaniola."

"He said you had better be able to produce permits for the guns and such from Panamá City or he might just turn you over to the police instead of simply throwing you off the comarca," Ernesto said in his excellent English. "You forfeit the weapons by even bringing them here."

"What the fucking hell! You ain't taking my stuff! I'll bring an army out to this hole and wipe the bunch of you gooks off the face of the earth!"

"Give it a go, asshole," Clint said. "You might find these people can make a game out of slicing the bunch of you into lunch meat."

"I know there ain't no such law! Every one of them has a machete!" another of them cried.

"And we didn't take the ten or twelve machetes you have in that monstrosity sitting out there. A machete is a tool on the comarca, not a weapon," Ernesto said reasonably. "They were told to take all weapons, and left them. That should tell an idiot they aren't weapons."

"You calling me a idiot?!" he snarled.

"No. Why should I state the obvious?" Ernesto replied.

The ass grabbed at Ernesto. He was at least twice his size. He got decked before he knew what hit him.

"The Indios will put up with a lot, but they won't be attacked," Clint said conversationally.

"Hell! that damned fucking ... they're a bunch of wimps! What the hell!?" the original one whined.

"Okay. You're right! This wimp just smacked this big brave macho stud in the puss. Want to be next?" Ernesto shot back.

"I suggest you take your three redneck asshole buddies back to wherever you came from and stay there until you learn to respect your betters," Clint said.

"Hey! You ain't no Indio! Where the fucking hell you get off with giving any orders, anyhow?" the original one said. "We came from Alabama – and Georgia. Danny. We just wanted to shoot some big game, but there ain't any."

"You think you can just go anywhere you like, treat people like slaves, shoot animals, and no one will care?" Clint asked. "You have a lot to learn."

"Look, I'm Sam Bills, he's Freddie Davis, that's Danny Watts, and he's Larry Tibbs. We can't let you keep our stuff. You know what the hell it cost?"

"I don't care what it cost. You don't have it in Panamá legally, and certainly not here on the comarca," Ernesto replied. "You don't take anything off the comarca Orlando says you don't. Clint is declared an Indio by Orlando here, and by Basilio, on the coast. They are the law. He is an Indio."

Clint started to say something, then thought it over. The two chiefs had said he was an Indio, in a way. Maybe that is the law.

"You got to be a Panamanian to be any Indio, and he ain't." Freddie said. "You better be careful who you fuck with. We can come get our stuff with the police."

"I see," Clint said. "You are going to get the police to come onto the comarca – incidentally, the police have no authority on the comarca unless Orlando personally calls them – to retrieve unpermitted weapons you brought into Panamá illegally. Neat!"

"Hey! All you do is slip some guy fifty bucks and they don't find nothing. All you have to do is slip another one fifty and they'll come get the stuff. The whole fucking country is on the take!"

"This ain't Panamá City, turkey. This is the comarca. You would have to bribe Orlando," Clint said, then turned to Orlando and asked (in the Indio language), "How much to let them take their stuff and go?"

Orlando laughed. "Oh, maybe a hundred million dollars and a couple of goodlooking gringas." Clint translated.

"I'll kick your fucking...." Freddie started. Clint interrupted him with, "One more threat and we keep the Hummer, too."

The four huddled and whined at each other for a minute.

Clint finally told them to get the hell off the comarca – now – or they really would keep the Hummer and turn them over to the police for illegal weapons as the cream on those strawberries.

"I'll see you around, fuckhead!" Sam snarled.

"Probably I'll see you in hell, someday," Clint returned. The Indios surrounded the four. Clint took several items from the pile of weapons and tossed them back into the Hummer. Larry started to reach for a machete when they got into the Hummer, but saw Clint standing there with eight or ten Indios, all of whom had machetes, while Clint still had the Glock, so thought better of it. He gave Clint the bird. Clint laughed.

They drove off.

"How many kilometers per gallon driving that thing?" Orlando asked.

"Ten, if you're lucky and going downhill," Clint replied.

"It'll cost them a hundred dollars to drive to David!" he cried. "How stupid!"

Clint laughed and said he'd hang around. The type would probably find some guns somewhere and come back at two in the morning.

They didn't come back, so Clint went on to Bocas Town in the morning – to find they went there. Sergio, head of violent crimes, met Clint at the dock to tell him some redneck asshole gringo had gotten his throat cut during the night. Something about a fight with Indios yesterday in Rambala or somewhere, according to one of his buddies.

"What? Some Indio came from Rambala and cut his throat while he was sleeping here in Bocas?" Clint asked.

"Sorta hard to swallow," Sergio agreed. "I think maybe they pulled that obnoxious act with the wrong person. Nobody seemed to like them, and two girls said they were almost raped by them. I think one of the girls' brothers or

something did it. Ben decked that one they call Danny –
the one who got his throat cut.

"I don't think Ben would kill anybody. They were
yelling that they hated queers and pushed at Ben. Bad
move! He should get the national citizenship medal,
whoever cut the SOB's throat! I won't try too hard to find
who did it."

"They were that bad?" Clint asked.

"Yeah. Ask Judi (Clint's neighbor, an attractive oriental
woman who helped Clint with many of his cases)," Sergio
answered. "I was ready to shoot the bunch of them,
myself. They thought they could come into the station and
order my men to go to Rambala and arrest a bunch of
Indios they couldn't identify for stealing their supplies
they wouldn't list."

"Not Rambala. The comarca – and it was Orlando and
Ernest, along with yours truly who confiscated a pile of
illegal weapons when they threatened people on the
comarca with them."

"Figures."

"I think I'll go home and take a long shower, then lay
around most of the day. Anymore trouble with that bunch
and I'll surprise them greatly when I walk in and you tell
them I'm with the police all over Panamá, as well as a
Ngobe Indio. You can ask exactly what kind of stuff was
kept by the Indios. That should make them happy!"

Sergio laughed. "You're the palest Indio I've ever seen.
They fell for that?"

"Orlando said he had declared that I'm Indio, he's the
chief, Basilio agreed with him;ergo I'm an Indio – by
law."

"Orlando said that? Then you are Indio and Panamanian.
Period. Caso permanente cerrado! That's the law. They
even have to give you a Panamanian passport."

"I thought that was good only on the comarcas."

"If you're a Ngobe Indio you are an indigenous Panamanian. The council declares it to be fact and there are no questions asked. I had a case while on duty in San Andreas. The jefe declared a German who was living on the comarca giving them free medical was a Cuna. He's a doctor. It went to Panamá City. The government didn't like it, but they had the constitution that says the indigenous populations are forever Panamanians. The Cuna are of the indigenous population. Dr. Schweiger is a Cuna. Dr. Schweiger is a Panamanian."

Clint grinned, waved, and headed for his house.

Judi Lum, Clint's neighbor, saw him from her deck over the bay, waved, and called a "Welcome home!" across the water to him on his deck. He waved back and said he'd come over. He had some questions about the dead redneck. She waved an invitation.

"This Danny Whatever – Watts – who got his throat sliced – what do you know about it?" Clint asked.

Judi made a sour face. "I didn't do it, but I sort of wish I had. There are four of them who are the most obnoxious redneck assholes I ever saw, including when I was living in the states for umpteen years. They never went anywhere without a can of beer in their hands. Serg had to come when the of guys patrolling told them to go inside or he'd dump them right there. They gave him a hard time, somebody called Serg, he came out and said to give him the beers. That Freddie bastard said he would give him the beer when he was big enough to take it.

"Serg put his pistol to the asses' head and said for all of them to give the officer their beers. The cop dumped them in the gutter. Serg said if they were seen with beer or anything else in the streets again his officers had orders to arrest them on the spot by whatever means necessary, including shooting them in the crotch.

"They went to the Toro Loco and were fairly quiet for a little while. They started getting boisterous and loud, so Natalie said they could go on their own or they could get tossed into the streets. Every man in the place stood up and came toward them. There were twelve or so, so they let discretion become the better part of valor for the first time in their lives.

"They went to The Reef and caused some trouble. They

went to the VIP and met their equals in the big badass category. They came back into town and saw Ben and Earl Somebody, his boyfriend for the last few nights, and started some kind of loud argument about queers in the streets.

"I don't know what happened. I think Ben kicked one of their asses. That's what I know."

"Danny, the dead one, shoved at Ben. Ben decked him. You know Ben."

"Ben ... wouldn't kill anybody while they were asleep. It wasn't him. He would beat them to death, maybe, but wouldn't use anything but his hands. He's big enough and good enough to do it."

"I guess one of his buddies did it," Clint said. "That ... wouldn't make sense. They're probably meek as rabbits unless the four are together. They spend their time trying to impress each other. Nobody else will put up with their crap. We get a few of the type, now and then."

Judi nodded. "You want me to see if anybody around here knows them?"

"I'd appreciate it. I don't know why they're here at all, much less why they're so intent in getting attention. It reminds me of another couple of assholes who were simply being a diversion."

"Puerto Armuelles. I remember that."

They chatted awhile, then Clint went home to clean up his e-mail and such, then to lay around for the rest of the day.

"Yo, Clint!" Ben greeted. "Que paso?"

Ben was a gay man who lived not far from Clint. They had become friends from the first.

"Not much. You cork that Danny character's bottle for him?"

"Not like that! I would sort of like to gut punch him to death, but he and his friends are such pathetic types."

"Yeah. I met them in the comarca."

"They were talking about some gringo who stole their equipment in Rambala. They didn't know his name. He sounded like you."

"Guilty as charged!" Clint replied. "It was a lot of illegal guns and such they took onto the comarca to threaten the Indios. They learned a little bit about the difference in Panamanian law and comarca law."

"Serg told me you're a Ngobe. Orlando, the chief, declared it, so it's set in titanium steel."

"Orlando and Basilio! You don't know how proud I am that they accept me that much!"

They chatted. Ben told Clint about the little confrontation. Clint agreed that they were the type who would be meek as rabbits if they weren't all there, so it wasn't likely one of them killed Danny. Clint said there was something a little off about them. They seemed almost to be acting.

He then laid around his place, fixed a few little things, such as a lock that was sticking because of the salt. He later cleaned up and went into town to talk to people. Judi called to say she and Ben were going to Refugio's. Dave was playing there with Curtis – if he showed up. Clint said he might drop in there later.

He went to the Nine Degrees for a very good meal, if a bit pricey. Just before he left, Sam, Freddie and Larry came in. They glared at him a bit, but didn't say anything to him.

He went to Refugio's and talked awhile with Judi, Ben and some overly-handsome bodybuilder type named Earl, who was with Ben. If it was anyone besides Ben, Clint would have avoided the type. This one seemed more a regular person without a bloated opinion of himself.

Manny Mathews, a retired mafia don from the states, came in with his wife to chat a bit. Clint met a girl from Denmark who was vacationing in Bocas for three days. They got along well. She stayed with him for the night – a very pleasant night.

Clint was laying in his hammock on his deck at five thirty with his second cup of coffee, waiting for the sunrise. Most of them were beautiful here. At about a quarter to six the light began to increase and the sky was dotted with rose-pink clouds that slowly turned to salmon, then to slightly reddish, but never turned into real red. It would be a nice morning.

Judi came onto her deck to water the orchids and waved and wagged a finger at him. He didn't bother to dress until he decided what he was going to do. He had on a jock strap this morning. Usually nothing.

Inga came sleepily onto the deck and waved to Judi. She asked Clint if he always came out there dressed like that in the morning.

"No. I usually don't wear the jock strap. Only when I have company."

They chatted for a few minutes. Inga was going to Bocas del Drago for the surf. Did he want to come along?

He said he had a few errands and a project or two. She said she was leaving Bocas on the five o'clock water taxi, so probably wouldn't see him before she left. She had a wonderful night.

Clint spent awhile, until seven, when some stores opened in town, sending e-mails to friends in Florida, California, and Panamá. He went into town, got groceries and supplies for a week or so, then headed back home. Sam, Freddie, and Larry were standing on the sidewalk by his gate. Clint sighed heavily and asked the cabbie to wait while he kicked a few asses. He got out.

"Faraday? We have to talk. No more shit," Sam said.

That surprised him. He nodded, paid the taxi, and grabbed the groceries. He led the trio inside. They didn't say much while he put the groceries away, then offered them coffee. Larry had a cup, the other two said they were nervous enough without caffeine.

"What's it about? The act on the comarca?" Clint asked.

"You knew that it was a act?" Sam asked. He seemed to be the spokesman for the trio. "I sort of wondered if you'd tumbled. We overdid it.

"I mean, we *are* what you call rednecks. We don't understand the kind of shit ... well, the shit people put up with. I guess we're bigtime bigots. We like our beer and our trucks and our guns and all that.

"This is how it came about. It was when we came into that place – Frontera. We stayed for that night in some hotel. Everybody said it was a dump, but it seemed Okay to us. It was a lot better than in some places, like in Nicaragua and Costa Rica. They ain't got much.

"We got a lot of money from ... a land deal in Georgia, and decided to see the world. At least some of it. Where we could go in our truck.

"The truck was part of our pay deal. It's great, but drinks gas like a elephant. It was costing us a lot more than we thought at first. I was sort of hoping the gooks would take the damned thing when we .. on that reservation. It would probably save us a fucking fortune.

"That's just talking. You don't give a fucking shit. I don't know how to talk to you.

"Alright. Straight out, like.

"We were at a place in Frontera, a little restaurant. We were trying to sell the fucking Hummer to get enough money to stay a couple days, then go home. Only the taxes if anyone bought it would take everything because ... you don't give a fuck. You know how that shit goes.

"We said we wanted to go to Bocas because some friends went there when they played some music – they have a band that's going places in Nashville. Local boys who made it, you know.

"Anyhow, this guy says he knows someone who would maybe give us a stake where we wouldn't need to sell the fucking thing. We could get it back to Georgia and sell it there if anybody was as stupid as we were and would even look at it.

"We knew he was right about that! We didn't get our shorts in a knot because he said we were stupid to buy the fucking thing in the first place. We *were*!

"Anyhow, he talked to this bird on his pocket phone and said it would be a day or two. All we had to do was go somewhere that was on the way to fucking Bocas, any-how. We would make who turned out to be you go away for a afternoon and night. He would pay us ten fucking grand.

"We said that was about as good as it gets! Who did we have to kill? He said that was the good part. We didn't have to kill anybody. Maybe kick your ass if that was the only fucking way to keep you there.

"We had to make it look like natural. You wasn't to ever know that's what we were doing.

"He said you really liked the gooks – sorry, Indians – and that you would be out there in a heartbeat if anybody tried to cause them trouble. He didn't tell us the part about the goo ... Indians having their own law, and that the government fuckheads wouldn't be able to take a hundred or so and forget it. We made him pay us for the guns and stuff when we got here.

"See, he paid five grand up front and five when we were

done. He paid like he said, but those guns cost us more than three grand, back in Louisiana. The guy who saw us in Frontera came to Bocas to pay. He said that was fair because he didn't tell us not to take any guns on the comaria ... whatever they call it.

"We thought everything was cool. We were going to stay here a week, then go to Colombia – only we couldn't take the fucking Hummer to Colombia – for a week, then to Brazil for a week, then home. He said not to spend much money here so we wouldn't be noticed, but we sort of got drunk and got in some shit with the cops. Lucky that captain or what-the-fuck-ever just dumped our beer and told us to stop the shit or get the fuck out.

"Then Danny started the shit about some queer and got knocked on his ass. Some queer kicked his ass and he didn't even get a lick in. That's hard to live down! He started running his mouth and some bigshit here heard it and said to be careful because this person we were working for is bad news if anybody causes his name to come out. Danny said we didn't fucking know the shit-head's name yet, but we would.

"I sort of explained that Danny sometimes has trouble holding his likker. He usually only drinks beer, but some asshole got him started on rum or seco or whatever they call it and he was a little wasted. We'd get him to the hotel and he'd sleep it off. Danny said he would go to the fucking hotel and shut his fucking mouth when he was goddamned good and ready, and not before. Freddie smacked him and said he was gonna cause us headaches. He always did when he got drunk. He'd go to the hotel now or get his stupid fucking ass kicked royally. Freddie can do it. He's done it before.

"Danny was still mouthing off, but we got him to the hotel and Freddie sort of put him to sleep. Not serious, but 'til the morning.

"Then he got his throat cut and we think maybe some badass we don't even know his name will come after us.

"See, if you know about it, there ain't no reason to come after us no more. If the fucking turkey just came and talked to us like a man 'stead of having to pay some fucking runner-boy to talk to us we'd make him see we ain't no problem. We said we'd keep clammed and we would keep fucking clammed, no matter what.

"That was before they trashed Danny. Now we just want to get out and go back to the states."

"Do you know who, the name of the person was who contacted you?" Clint asked.

"We just called him Pedro, but I don't think that's his name," Sam answered.

"I heard some guy call him Nando," Larry volunteered. "That guy by the big supermarket they call Juli – I mean the guy, not the store – Juli, for – but I don't think he's queer. He don't act like it."

"His name's Julio. It's a common name here," Clint said. "So I can find out what it's about. You'd be smart to get as far away from here as fast as you can. If it's the Russian mafia or the Mexican mafia this *ain't* the country you want to be in." (He said that to scare them. There wasn't much chance they were involved in anything like this.)

"That cop, the fucking captain-shit who dumped our beer, said we couldn't go nowhere 'til he said so," Freddie said. "I only want to get out of this fucking hole of a country. We don't fit here. I don't never know what the fucking hell is going on!"

"I think I can get them to let you go if you leave the country fast. They don't want trouble from those people," Clint said. "I work with the police. Those mafia types tie up the whole department, and the courts are afraid of them and will let them go, even when they're convicted."

Larry and Freddie both groaned. Sam looked surprised. "You mean some asshole set us up to keep a fucking cop away from where they were doing...! Fucking goddamned *shit*! You're a fucking *cop*?!"

"Sort of. How fast can you be out? I have to give him so many hours before they pick you up. You would go, but they'd keep everything you have, including money, except to pay for your flight home."

"I can't get on no plane! I won't never get on no fucking plane!" Freddie whined.

"We can get out in ... is there someplace near here? I heard there is. To Costa Rica," Sam said.

"Changuinola to Sixola and cross. I guess they can get that monster across. The roads are bad in Costa Rica, but that thing will take them."

"How long?" Larry asked.

"You left the Hummer in Almirante?" Clint asked. "Water taxi to Almirante, one more hour. Almirante to Changuinola, one hour. It'll take less, but you have to have some bit of leeway. Changuinola to the border, thirty minutes, two hours of passport and paper handling this side.

"You can be out by three if you leave in an hour. I'll get Sergio to allow you until six tonight.

"Listen! Do *not* tell anyone you're going. Let them think you're just going to Changuinola to shop because you heard they have everything there and it's cheap as all hell. You can be gone before they suspect anything. They wouldn't expect you back here before five or six, anyhow."

They agreed. Clint went to town separate from them so no one would connect that they were at his place. They would tell people they went to the beach, but it sucks.

They wouldn't cancel the hotel. They'd say they were going shopping and would be back.

Clint talked to Sergio and told him basically that they were set up. It would be far better to let them go than it would be to have a couple more of them killed in Bocas Town. Sergio agreed. He had an officer contact them, ostensibly to ask some questions, and tell them they had to get out fast and the way Clint Faraday suggested.

Clint went out to see if he could find Juli.

Clint couldn't find Juli, so he went home. Judi called to say he should come over for a snack.

"I found out a little, but not much," Judi said over the hojadres and pollo aguisada. "Juli Williams was talking to a man called Fernando about the one who was killed. I said that was interesting. Did he know where anyone had some decent carne?

"He said the backstreet China and that Nando was connected with some big money man in Panamá City and was here on some kind of deal to do with the one who had his throat cut.

"I said it wasn't smart to get tied up with those kind of people and did he see the big tuna Maxi caught?

"Do you any good?"

That was Judi's method. Cause a comment by dropping a name or something, then act like it was only a comment and change the subject. Then the person will try to impress her with what they know. It always seemed to work – with her.

"It confirms some things. I have to know who this Nando is."

"Fernando Selamas. Dona was talking with him at the Laguna and I stopped to ask her how her mother's doing. She's in the hospital. She sort of had to introduce him."

"You're amazing."

"He works for some guy who owns a trucking company. Freight haulers. All over Central America. He gave me his card, which was why Dona didn't really want to introduce us."

Judi is very attractive and exotic, with her oriental heritage.

Judi gave Clint a business card. Eugenio Taylor Transport Systems, S.A.

Clint shook his head. That would save him a week and a lot of travel. Now he wanted to know exactly what a transport company was transporting that would get his specific attention.

He waited until he had figured part of it clearly, then called Manny. Manny could get all kinds of information through his contacts. This one, he didn't know much about, but would try to find the information.

Clint then went back to town. The Larry, Curly, and Mo Trio, as he thought of them, were gone. Sergio had them discretely followed and they were between Ojos de Agua and Changuinola. Another car was following them, so Sergio had the follower stopped for an insurance and license check when he passed in an illegal zone (which everyone did. It was usually ignored, but was an excuse – seeing the police truck was two cars behind.).

That would work out well. It would be easier to learn things with them gone. Though it wouldn't be intentional this time, they would still be a distraction.

Nando was in the parque with Dona, sitting on a bench. Clint thought of saying something to him, then thought better of it. Wait until the trio were out of the country. He waved to Dona and kept on walking. He went to the dock, thought about it for a few minutes, then went home and got his boat to go to Almirante and to the ferry offices.

"Did Eugenio Taylor Transport bring in anything or take out anything the past three days?" he asked.

Jorge checked the manifests and shrugged. "Not for about two weeks, if I remember. They took a load in and a load out. Trucks loaded both ways."

Clint thanked him and went to the compound where they kept the trucks, but Taylor didn't leave anything there.

Where? What kind of stuff did they generally carry?

He went to Ojos de Agua. Taylor didn't handle anything there. That eliminated construction materials. The card didn't say anything about a specialty.

He went to Changuinola. Taylor sometimes brought refrigerators, washers, and such to the bigger stores. Nothing for two weeks or so.

The other ... Sixola? Contraband through Costa Rica?

A quick trip. No. They didn't come to Sixola.

Chiriqui Grande. They delivered regularly to several places there. They stopped in Mali and points between. They sometimes went to Punta Pena and Rambala.

Was that a connection?

Possibly. Probably. That's why whoever knew he went to the comarca fairly often and that he would move to protect the Indios so fast.

He had another idea and went back to Chiriqui Grande and to the aduana. Taylor sometimes picked up loads from the docks there. Mostly furniture items from Colombia and the Caribbean islands. They carried loads to be taken to those places.

Whatever came in was very carefully checked. What went out was sealed and seldom checked. That was the job of wherever the stuff was delivered.

They were taking something out of Panamá. What?

It would be a matter of finding where the stuff was picked up. The major transshippers were in David, Santiago, and Panamá City. Maybe directly from Colon, but this was going out, so that wasn't likely.

So. David was closest. He caught the next bus.

Clint booked into the Pension Costa Rica, then, as it was getting late, went to dinner at La Tipica, then to Peter's place in the Hotel Iris to mingle and chat with people. Not much was new, and tomorrow might be long and hard, so he went back to the Costa Rica and had a good night's sleep. In the morning, at daybreak, he went to four places where the drivers hung out when they were in town for a night to wait for tomorrow's loads. There were two Taylor trucks near Brother Bar, parked down the street. Chiriqui was playing Herrera at the nearby stadium, and the drivers had gone there last night, stayed at the nearby hostel, and would be in about seven thirty to get the trucks to be loaded. They were usually loaded at terminal #3 or #4. These would be at #3 or they would have stayed over by the fairgrounds.

Okay. If this was the pickup point, it would be stuff brought in from the area of Chiriqui and kept in the warehouses until it was picked up. So far as Clint knew, there wasn't anything worth this mess anywhere in Chiriqui.

Next stop, Santiago! The bus left on the hour. He could get the 9:00 bus and be in Santiago by 1:00. That would leave him time to come back ... unless he had to go on to Panamá City.

He sighed, went to a local restaurant for a good break- fast, then to the pension for his bag, then to the bus.

Santiago is laid back and lazy on the outskirts. Cattle country, though a lot of government business was handled there.

Trucking permits? It was an idea.

He checked places Taylor picked up stuff. Only Lopez Storage. They hadn't picked up anything going toward Bocas in two weeks.

Clint went to the registro to check the permits issued lately. Taylor had nothing from Panamá City for several days. They picked up a load in Santiago that was for

Bocas Province. Household appliances. That could mean he had to concentrate on David. Back there.

He went to transhipping terminal #3. Taylor had picked up a load of appliances there in the time frame. The other terminal, #4, they picked up a load of boxes labeled household items. It was left for them from a Taylor truck eight days before.

Back to #3. The stuff was left by three wholesalers from Panamá City and Colon.

#4 was most likely. Leave whatever for a few days so there wouldn't be apparent connection. Clint wanted to know what was really in those boxes. It wasn't household items!

He waited around until lunch break and talked to the loader operators. They didn't remember anything about Taylor. It was just "Load pallets in section four B" on the Taylor truck.

Clint thought, then went to where the dispatch director was eating. He was about twenty, and said his name was Luis. He just checked off the stuff as it was loaded or unloaded.

"You note which trucks delivered and which ones picked up?" he asked.

"Sure. Takes a genius! I need the work until I can find a decent job, though it pays well enough. I can't gripe."

"Could I see the records from eight days ago?"

"With a legal order or if you're a cop or something."

"I'm police. National. Check with Panamá City or Bocas Town."

"Good enough for me. I'll be back in about forty five minutes."

Clint thanked him and had a fair meal, then walked around for a few minutes before he went back to the terminal. Luis dug through some files and handed him a sheet before going out to check a load going out. He could find whatever he needed in the files.

The stuff came from some local furniture manufacturers. There were seventy nine boxes, each with a code number. On the third.

Clint sat back. He looked at the manifests for Taylor (Luis said they were in the files. Look at what you want, but don't take anything) trucks loaded in the past four days. Just one. Eighty four boxes. What? Five boxes appeared through teleportation?

He looked at the loading manifest and noticed an asterisk with a notation that the boxes were added seven days before.

Clint checked the manifests for Taylor loads on that date. Five boxes from Tole. Carried in by an independent carrier called L&L&L&L Cargo.

That would be it. He went to the registro and used the computers to check out L&L&L&L. Four brothers and sisters who sometimes carried a load locally.

Clint had noted something else about the loading manifest. The asterisk was in the middle, not at either end.

Why? So it would be buried in the middle of the load? There was an access door near the front and the loading one in the rear. This would put the boxes where no one could reach them easily. They would have to unload a lot of things to find them.

Veddy interesdink. This was what it was about – but what was that?

Clint was headed back to the pension when his phone buzzed. He answered. It was Sergio. The man stopped when he was following the trio was dead. He had his throat cut in Changuinola.

"Where was ... but I thought ... where was Nando Selamas?"

"Nando Selamas? Who is he – and why would I know?"

"Sorry. It's just a name that may or may not be connected. I'll check him out and let you know if there's a connection."

When he hung up he called Judi. She said Nando had gone to Almirante at about two thirty yesterday. He was back in Bocas Town now.

Clint called Sergio. The follower, Santo Santos, was killed last night after six thirty and before seven.

"Were the trio gone?"

"For about two hours. That's when they crossed into Costa Rica, after the papers check."

Clint sat back to think. Nando was who he figured for Danny's killer, but why would he kill the one he had following them?

Because he didn't have that one following them, stupid! This was getting complicated.

Okay. He was set up for delay on the twelfth. The stuff had been in the warehouse, ready, for six or seven days. They waited for a time Clint would be occupied while they moved the stuff. It was loaded in Chiriqui Grande on the twelfth and sailed later on the twelfth or early the thirteenth.

This was strange! Why would he even know about whatever it was – or care?

It came from the Tole area. What was there? Who was the follower working for? Maybe that would give him a hint. He needed about anything to be able to connect anything else. All he had was a lot of disjointed anecdotal information, in effect.

He called Manny. Manny couldn't get anything more than he had. Taylor seemed to be clean, at least from anything big. He would check on Santo Santos.

Clint went back to the pension. He didn't have a hint of

a direction. He thought for awhile, then decided his only hope of learning anything was Tole. He was about to go to the bus when Manny called to say Santos seemed to be a sort of semi-wannabe detective with delusions that it was like TV. With him dead, it would be hard to find who he was working for. "They're doing a good job of covering their tracks."

"A very professional kind of job," Clint agreed. "Makes you wonder. Maybe they want something and this is a distraction in layers."

They chatted a bit, then Clint went to the bus.

Tole is a tranquil little place near the Pacific. Clint liked that kind of place. Many of the people here were Indios, though not Ngobe. Not much was the same in their language.

He checked around for quite some time, but didn't learn much. L&L&L&L were about six kilometers away and usually only carried local vegetables and such for friends or would carry other things when someone moved or bought something that was delivered to the warehouse. He went to find L&L&L were working in the finca, but L was there.

"It's Lopez and Lopez and Lopez and Lopez. We're three brothers and one sister. We bought the truck together and run the finca together," Esmeralda Mendez Lopez explained. "We don't do much with that part. Maybe once or twice a week, and local.

"I remember that part, though. A man who has a big finca in Veraguas brought it and paid us to take it to David when we were going with something else. He said it wasn't anything but stuff from a relative, a cousin, who was moving to Bocas and would have to store it until he had a house, anyway. No hurry, but as soon as they could.

"We had some things from Santiago to David for the next morning, so took it.

"Quentin! His name was either Martin Quentin or Quentin Martin! I remember, because it was sort of unusual.

"It was real. His cedula said the same thing."

"Oh, then you have his cedula (national ID card) number?"

"Oh, sure. It's the law. We have to get your cedula and

signature." She went inside and came out with a slip of paper with the name and number. That might help a lot in finding who he was. The total weight of five boxes was twenty two kilos. They were marked fragile, though there was a note that it wasn't really very fragile. That was already on the used boxes, so they wouldn't require insurance, and wouldn't hold L&L&L&L accountable for any damage.

Tole was near the coast, so it could well be something brought in, which still didn't quite make sense to Clint. Why would it be brought there, then shipped by truck, then transhipped by truck to be loaded on a ship in Chiriqui Grande? It was obvious enough that somebody wanted it to be untraceable, but how and why was Clint Faraday involved to the point he had to be distracted while they were doing it? It could easily have been set up to be delivered to David that day – if the stuff from Santiago was there to be sure the stuff from Veraguas went that day. Clint didn't want to appear too absorbed with it, so didn't ask who had the other part of the delivery set up.

Veraguas. Santiago. He was halfway there, so caught the next bus. Clint grinned and headed for the bus. He was going to throw a few curves, himself!

Santiago and to the registro. He checked on Quentin Martin, to find he ran a large cattle ranch for Kelvin Taylor. There was a connection if Clint didn't have a least clue as to what was connected. Taylor and the trio and Taylor behind Nando. That there was a connection was obvious. The question was; How is Clint Faraday involved in the mess? Why?

Two murders – that he knew about. Some idiot rednecks paid to distract him (from what?). Shipments all over the western end of Panamá. An apparently hired killer in

Bocas Town.

This was stupid! What in *hell* was going on? What the *hell* was in those boxes?

They had gone to some expense with this. Ten thousand just to distract him a couple of hours. Shipping and transhipping boxes. No argument about paying for the seized guns – but kill some redneck gringo because he was talking about it?

The other murder. The follower. He should be checking him instead of Nando. Maybe the connection was there. Reasoning it out, there were two groups involved, probably groups who didn't like each other or who had to be stopped from something.

Reason it further. He had to be distracted, then ... Manny was right. It was a layered distraction. This running around was a distraction. That meant the real solution was with Santos, not this bunch.

Reason it even further. There wasn't anything in those boxes. There isn't anything to be found in western Panamá.

Maybe there was! No way around it, the Taylors were in it up to their ears! He knew that the Taylors weren't there. Martin was running the ranch. Taylor wasn't there. The Taylor family was large and found all over Panamá. Clint knew several in Bocas Town. They were too often involved in political jobs, for a large part.

This wasn't politics. Was it?

No. There wouldn't be any reason to distract Clint over politics. He didn't care.

He went back to David on the next bus. They definitely were leaving clues that would take him to Panamá City. That was where they were, so they wanted him to come there, but only after he followed this thing to this point.

Judi called and said Nando had asked her about him. "He

said he wanted to talk to you about a business deal. I told him you went somewhere and didn't leave any message as to where. It seems as if he's supposed to warn you about something."

"I think he wants to warn me about some people who want to warn me about him," Clint replied. "I have a little of this worked out, I think. It's a mess, in some ways. I just can't figure what I have to do with anything.

"Judi, maybe we should try to find who was in Bocas Town or Almirante on the twelfth. There was someone who was scheduled to be there ... but they didn't ... they waited until I was close enough to be distracted. That still means they were in Bocas Town or Almirante on the twelfth, but probably for a day or two before, and maybe they still are.

"Who's in town for a couple of days before the twelfth and maybe a day or two more?"

"Other than the regular tourists, nobody who sticks out. I can check. It's obvious there's big money involved, so those people are easy to check.

"Clint, there's been a big yacht sitting by the channel for several days. I think it left on the thirteenth. I thought of it because some people asked if it was Jimmy Buffet's yacht, but it isn't. He doesn't stay long when he's here, and it was there for a week."

"See what you can find out about it. It may be my connection."

They chatted a few minutes, then Clint relaxed for the rest of the trip. They were out of celular range, anyhow.

When they reached David, Clint stretched and headed for Pedrigal. He had a friend there who said he could stay anytime. She had two bedrooms that were never used – that he wouldn't use, either. That would be the last place they would expect him to go. It might be a good idea to disappear for a day or two to see who was looking for him. He probably wasn't followed yet. It was possible enough that he simply walked along the street until a Pedrigal bus came by and flagged it when it stopped for a stop sign, jumped on, and it kept going. If he was being followed the only choice the follower had was a taxi.

This was the bus that went past the airport. Clint sat in the back and noted that a taxi was hanging back about a block when they reached the main road. He got off at the airport and the taxi turned in there half a minute later and went on to the terminal. Clint went back out and across the road, then down a side street. The follower got off at the terminal, which Clint could see from there, and was hanging around out front, watching the entrance road for him to come walking in.

Surprise! He wouldn't be walking in.

The follower could see the main road from where he was. There were a couple of women waiting for a bus, so Clint managed to step into view as the bus approached. It stopped, the two women got on, Clint walked back and was able to dodge down the side street while the bus blocked the view. The follower was wildly trying to flag a cab. Clint laughed and went on down the side street to stroll the eight blocks to Irina's place.

"Mr. Faraday? This is Vasily Armakov. We met briefly in Panamá City two years ago."

Clint had answered a buzz from an "unknown" number. "Yes?"

"I believe you have been drawn into something that is very nasty. I fear it may have been my fault. I want to warn you that the people who are behind this are very dangerous. Both sides – and there are two."

"I see. What's it really about?"

"The supply of certain ... implements that are designed for one purpose, but are to be used for another purpose. I am trying to stop the delivery of those items."

"It was your yacht in the bay at Bocas?"

"No. I think perhaps that was only a vessel that was there. They are simple tourists or something as mundane. They have nothing to do with this.

"Mr. Faraday, I have nothing to do with it, except to stop it. My homeland is part of what is at risk. It is representatives of two other countries. They are trying to ... promote a thing that will enslave one culture to another. My home merely happens to be too close in the area. If either is successful we are at risk. They will not stop with subjugation of one by the other. It will make them feel invincible."

"Both in the old Soviet Block?"

"Yes. I will not say more about that. It is just that a statement made by myself in surprise may have made you appear to be a deadly danger to both adversaries. I merely said, upon being informed of the action by one, that you were in Bocas and would act to prevent such a travesty, should you become aware of it, and that you are very capable.

"I do not know if they have ... if they have done more than to delay your knowledge of them. I feel you are intelligent enough to have discerned that is what is happening."

"It was your man following me?"

There was a short pause. "So you detected him. He was much better than the opposition men. I have him there for your protection. There were two others. One is dead, and one is in Bocas."

"Yeah. Fernando Salamas. He killed Santos."

"I would imagine that is the train of events. He is very

possibly ordered to kill you if you seem to be getting too near the truth."

"I need more information. I can't do anything if all I know is Taylor is part of it."

"Taylor is an idiot. He thinks he's making a deal where he gets some millions of dollars. He will get dead, should he fulfill the obligation he thinks he has entered into. These people want no trail for anyone to follow. They have made a terrible mistake in getting you involved, and know it. Now they fear you will have left something somewhere that will implicate them. Had they not been introduced to that possibility, they would have eliminated you from the first, not delayed you. There is another place where you are known that has them very afraid. I do not know where that place is or why they so fear you."

"Thanks."

"It would be wise for you to actually leave something that indicates you know much more than is truth. Preferably where they can get a copy. It can suggest far more than you do know. Mention Niklev, Feinberg, Ghenkof, and Fandrev. Those names will strike a mutual fear into them. They will have to tread very carefully down any path where those names might be revealed. It will guarantee that they will do little more than try to intimidate you until they have the mis ... shipment. You need only leave the names somewhere. Do not try to build a scenario with them doing anything. It would show that you know little or nothing."

"Yeah. I really don't know anything."

"You are far safer not knowing."

"Not my nature. I'll dig into it, but just to the extent it affects people here. Their worst mistake with me was bringing the Indios into it. Me? Who cares. My friends? I'll never let it go."

"Yes. I agree. I was most surprised to find that you are Ngobe."

"They're my people."

"Yes. You have made them so. I respect that more than you can know. I must go." He hung up. Clint sat back to think, then made a list of people and what he'd learned. He added a few more to make them wonder what the hell he was doing. Turn about's fair play!

He put the four names Armakov gave him into the list that he was supposedly checking on through the internet. They were at separate points, and he put a question mark after each. They'd also have to wonder why the names were in those positions.

He slightly crumpled the papers so they'd look used and dropped the notes into his backpack.

He decided, seeing he was here, he would spend the rest of the day and the night there.

He went back into David just before noon and checked into the Costa Rica. Now that he knew he could spot the one besides Armakov's man, so would make it easy for him to find the note. He put the backpack in his room and went to lunch at the Hotel Alcala'. They had better than average meals, moderately priced.

He walked around a bit, greeting people, then went back to the pension. The little traps he set showed that his backpack had been searched. Now he had a bit of a weird dilemma. The other follower had followed him to the Alcala' hotel. Armakov's man didn't, unless he was better at it than Clint believed.

Something else to consider. Clint laid on the bed to think. A grin slowly moved across his face.

He had kept Armakov's cel number. He never got rid of one. It took about ten minutes to find it, then he called.

"Yes, Mr. Faraday? – and how did you get this number?"

"He did. You gave it to me two years ago, in the golf club."

Armakov laughed. "So you figured all along that I was trying to find the leak there. Eladio Camacho, my good loyal man."

"Yeah. You wouldn't have to call me if you knew where they got what you said about me."

"You're very sharp, Mr. Faraday. I am highly impressed. You had me believing I had you fooled about my true aim. I assure you, I also meant to warn you, even though I felt it was not necessary to do so.

"There will soon be another there to follow you."

"Not needed. I can take care of myself. Right about now, they're wondering what I found about the names on the internet. I made it look like a list several days old and put information about all of the people except those four on the list with some references to search engines I use. All I put by those names – and I spread them through the list – was a question mark."

"So they will wonder how you found the names and what you may have learned since the list was written. I am again impressed. They will spend inordinate time trying to find their own leaks. I hope you didn't put any names that do not deserve the attentions of those people.

"Call me Vasily. May I call you Clint?"

"Of course. I'm surprised you didn't from the first."

They talked for a couple more minutes about good restaurants, then Clint rung off.

What now? Wait? Or actually see what he could learn about those names?

He called Manny.

Manny said he could figure who Feinberg was, and maybe Ghenkof. He'd see if there was any information out that might tie them into anything other than the regular rackets. He called Judi, but there wasn't anything new to report. It seemed that Nando was gone. Sergio had word out that he needed to have a heart-to-heart with the man. Besides which, Clint was gone off into the sunset somewhere.

He borrowed Bob's laptop and went on the wireless internet. He checked his e-mail and such, then started looking for the names.

The trouble with that kind of search, where he only had part of the name, was that the comp came up with hundreds of Niklev, fifty or so Ghenkof and fifty or so Fandrev. It came up with more than a thousand Feinberg. Clint knew that search would be as much as hopeless. He could only read through to see if anything clicked.

He spent about two hours on it, then went out to walk around town. Not much new was going on. David is a laid-back city that is more like a large town. People would stop to chat and trade gossip, seldom mean. While he was wandering, he went to the bazaar strip and bought new underwear and supplies, along with some light shirts and other clothing that was about a third of the price the same thing cost in Bocas Town.

Manny called and said there wasn't much about his people, but that Feinberg was getting very cozy with some big arms dealers in the Far East. He seemed very interested in guided missiles.

Clint remembered what Vasily almost said. It connected, in a way. What the *hell* did Panamá have to do with it?

They sure as sunset didn't ship any missiles from Chiriqui Grande or Bocas del Toro or anywhere else in Panamá! He didn't even know where to begin.

Okay. Financing was all it could be. They were smuggling something out of Panamá. What? It wasn't drugs. That wouldn't be handled in that area. It would more likely come from Colombia in bulk. What was in Panamá that would turn that kind of money?

There were a few mines for silver and lead. There was some zinc. Not enough to finance anything vaguely like what was needed to buy a missile. Gold was 99% a scam. There just wasn't that much on that order here. What oil was here couldn't be smuggled anywhere. How do you smuggle ten million barrels of oil?

If you had a ton of silver and John Doe had ten tons of lead and Mary Smith had fifty pounds of gold ... it still wasn't anywhere close to what they needed. What could there be that would finance something like this?

He decided to call his weird musician friend, Dave. Dave said the only thing it could be is money. Panamá is famous for laundering. It was something that would get Clint's attention.

"It wouldn't get my attention if I didn't know about it," Clint pointed out.

"Didn't you just say they got your attention by accident or something?"

"Oh, shit!"

"Sort of intriguing. A few hundred million in cash put on a boat and shipped to somewhere else to be put on a boat. I could come up with a few stories with that as a background! The types it would involve would make it a great basic for a blood-and-guts, what they call 'action' book."

"There are enough types in this already. Thanks. I didn't

see the obvious, again."

"As Merlin Tyana says, step back. You're too close to it. You can't see the whole picture from that close, only bits and pieces."

"Who the hell is ... never mind. A character in those books you write."

They chatted a bit, then Clint called Manny.

"How much money is being shipped out of here by those people?"

There was a pause. "That's an angle I wouldn't have considered. I'll see if there's anything to it – but whoever's behind it seems to be very professional. Have you found out what it's about?"

"Buying missiles."

"No shit? That would explain Feinberg. He might have the connections for it. They won't be nuclear."

"That's what has me worried. A few regular missiles wouldn't change the balance."

"It would depend on where they're aimed."

They talked for a bit, then Clint called Judi.

"Hi. How're things in Glock-amora?"

"Same old same old. Hi, Clint."

"Jude, what have you heard, if anything, lately about money laundering?"

"Not a lot, but nobody mentioned anything to get me curious. I can check. There's always a lot of that here."

"I'm not talking about a few pitiful millions."

"Oh? Now I'm curious!"

They talked about the weather and local news, then Clint sat back to, as Dave suggested, "Step back" to try to see the whole picture.

It was still blurry – *my god! Did I really come up with that?*

An hour later he had a new scenario figured, but it still

didn't make much sense. Cash would come from the offshore banks, not interior Panamá. It seemed less and less likely. Something was missing. Something major.

The phone rang. It was Manny.

"Clint? I got some word about one of your people. Fandrev. He's a nuclear scientist. Help anything?"

"Hell no! Shit fire! That brings up a very scary possibility."

"The missiles they're going after are guided and fairly accurate, but they deliver standard payloads – so maybe that's what they're doing. By the time they've set it up to where it's operational, the payload wouldn't be standard anymore."

"But ... it still doesn't make any sense! Why am I involved? What could I know that would make them try to keep me out, but would make them afraid ... because I could connect Fandrev to missiles.

"Could they get the stuff to make them nuclear anywhere?"

"I don't know that much about it. Call Dave. He wrote some stuff about nuclears some years ago. Maybe he can add two and two and come up with something more than zero."

"You're as bad as he is – or me."

"Judi told me about your Glock-amora remark. Lame!"

"Hah! You don't know lame! Try `looking at the picture, but it's blurry' for size!"

"That's downright sick!"

Clint agreed and called Dave, who was out in the town. He left a message to call him back.

He walked around the quieter parts of David to think, stopping in the Luz Rosa for a bit of the very good local food there.

No matter how you added it, it was scary, and was pretty

close to impossible, according to what he knew about nuclears – which approached zero. He was walking back toward the pension when Dave called and asked what he wanted.

"Dave, is it possible to convert a standard-type guided missile to nuclear? Could a few people who knew something about nuclears do it? Is it even possible?"

"Oh, yeah! To make a really dirty type, it's not only possible, it's easy. All you need is enough fuel."

"Fuel? What...?

"Uranium. Plutonium. Get two half-critical masses, set them far enough apart that they don't initiate a reaction, slap them together, and boom. Radiaoactive particles for miles, and a big hole where it went off."

"Cripes!"

"I sincerely hope you're simply theorizing about some idiotic action book you read or something. I very sincerely hope that you're letting your imagination roam out in left field."

"And Manny says I'm bad?"

"Yeah. That one even gets a groan from me."

It still didn't make sense. What did Panamá have to do with anything? Why was he involved, from any angle? What did he know – or what did they *think* he knew that brought him into it, in the first place?

It was time to stop wandering all over the place with this. It wasn't a game. He had to organize his thought and stop doing the random facts bit. That wasn't working.

They would have to be able to connect him to something in the past to be worried about him in any way now. What had happened in the past that they would worry about?

They weren't shipping laundered cash out. That was stupid to have ever contemplated. That was done every day, and easily. They weren't trying ... the money was secondary or less.

That left the, as Dave called it, fuel. There weren't any reactors that produced plutonium in Panamá. Clint knew enough about nuclears to know that. Those breeder reactors always got international attention. That left, so far as Clint knew, uranium. Maybe radium?

Clint didn't know if there was any uranium in Panamá. He went to the internet to check it out. Not in sufficient quantity that had been located.

While he was there he checked on where it was found and under what conditions. It was found in areas where there were other heavy metals. Gold, silver, lead, thallium, mercury, platinum.

There was some mercury in Panamá, a little gold, and more silver. Plenty of lead.

Clint had one case where a lode of lead was found on the finca of a friend. There was a little silver there, too. And zinc. Was there any uranium? Had anyone even checked?

That was all he could think of that could tie him into it.

Why would they believe he knew about it if they found uranium there? Because he had made a show of knowing how to read sonic mapping and mining procedures in that oil dome that was actually sulfur?

That was just inside the line of a likely wrong assumption.

How to bring them out?

He called Armakov. "Do you know what it's about? No bullshit!"

"Clint? I ... not really. They ... I don't at all like the combination coming together. Feinberg, missiles, and a scientist. I find it terribly disturbing that they reacted the way they did. I don't know why."

"Okay. I know about Fandrev and Feinberg. What or who are the others?"

"Ghenkof is a sort of shady fringe character into protection and security. He protects thugs, for the most part. He's one himself. KGB. Gregor Ivan Niklev, I can't figure, other than a possible money man. I don't know his background."

"I can find it, I think. I have a source or two."

"What is it about?"

"I'm not sure, but it's very scary."

"Let me know? Facts?"

"Certainly." He hung up. It was always abrupt with Armakov.

Internet again. He knew enough to be able to find something, he hoped. Gregor Ivan Niklev.

There were nine. Two were engineers, which might be the connection. The others were in different fields.

What kind of engineers?

Structural and extraction.

Extraction. Extract uranium.

Another search engine came up with seven, the extraction engineer not among them. The third and last one he checked came up with the same seven. The only reason the one he figured was on the first was his University of Moscow degree listing. 1974. He would be around 55 years old. He hadn't excelled at anything to the point he was noted on the net.

There had to be another, unless they found out about the uranium by accident. Probably, a lot of people went around the areas where heavy metal deposits were found to check the area with Geiger counters or something. If it was on private property there was a good chance only one had searched for it wherever it was found.

How to find out where the lode was?

Time to head for Puerto Armuelles. That would certainly get someone's attention!

So. Use a disguise.

What?

The older proper Spanish-looking man got off the bus and stretched his back, swore mildly, and limped around for a few steps to get circulation going again in his legs. He asked, in very proper Spanish, where there might be an acceptable hotel, and was directed to Central.

Clint had stayed there many times. This guy had to be told where it was. A local man, Basilio, said it was the building across the square. The man pointed his thin black cane at the building, and Basilio nodded. The man thanked him.

He went to the station and requested that they hold his two large suitcases there until he found lodging. They said that was the custom.

The man went into a local restaurant and sat at a back table to take his folding reading glasses from their leather case to read the menu in the card holder in the center of the table. He decided to have the pescado aguisada with yuca and lechuga. He snapped his fingers for the waitress, then apologized when she came over, explaining that was the custom in Madeira. Lana, who Clint knew well, said that it was no big deal. Different people had different customs. He asked what the custom was here. She said she looked around all the time. When she looked his way, put his hand up. He thanked her.

The food here was good, as Clint knew. His disguise was good, if Lana or Basilio didn't see through it. He ate the meal, left a large propina, and went to the hotel to ask that they send someone for his luggage, then went to his room. He was liked for his proper pleasant manner and his obvious respect for other people, and was given one of the best rooms with a balcony that looked over the parque to the Pacific.

Clint laid on the bed for about an hour, then went to ask where he might find interest in the town. Jeraldo, at the desk, said it would depend on what he was looking for. The muelle was popular, there were the usual collection of bars, there was a brothel, El Critico, just out of town, that was popular and higher class.

Clint knew the place. As an unaccompanied Spaniard, he would be expected to go to such places. A lot of information could be gathered there, as he knew from former visits.

He walked out to the pier and chatted with the very friendly people. He told them he was looking for a place in Panamá to retire. He found it was a better place than Europe. The people made the difference. Panamanians were, for the most part, the most amiable people he had met in his travels over much of the world. He wanted to live in a place where people liked and respected one another. Where people had time to chat and exchange experiences. He gave the name of Generoso Morales.

He spent some time on the pier, talking to several people he knew well. One, Enrique Silva, an Indio from Bocas, seemed to be interested more than the others in him. When they were walking back toward the shore, Clint asked why.

"Because I'm very sure you are a friend I know," he said in Guayme, the Indio language in Bocas del Toro.

"I hope I am a friend. I am honored that you would say so."

"Then you are that friend."

Clint smiled and nodded.

"I know there is a reason for this, so I will never let anyone know."

Clint nodded again. They were getting close to a group who were standing near the entrance. Enrique said he was pleased to have met Sr. Morales, and hoped they would meet soon again, and went up the road to the right. Clint nodded, and said, "Buenos!" to the group and headed back toward the hotel.

He strolled around town a bit more, went to his room, cleaned up, and put on another suit, went to the brothel, El Critico, for a delicious meal and to talk to a number of the locals. The women there were mostly from Colombia, and Clint paid the forty dollars to spend an hour with one beautiful girl in the cabins out back, as would be expected of anyone from the culture in Spain. He was able to learn there were a few Russian people in town a week or so ago. One of them stayed at a rented house near the beach. She had gone there once, but didn't like the way the man, Ivan, treated her. She wasn't a dog or cow to be ordered in and out as her master chose. The girls didn't like him, but he paid well.

He went back to the hotel and asked Jeraldo if he could have a taxi there in the morning early, say 8:30, to take him around the nearby countryside so he could learn more of the place. He liked Puerto Armuelles very much. Perhaps he would retire in the area. A man could do far worse.

The taxi driver said there wasn't much along the road toward Costa Rica, except for some fincas and a silver mine. No one was allowed on the silver mine. The Indio who owned the property was a very friendly sort who did a lot to help the locals with medical and education. Everyone called him "amigo." The whole family were liked.

Clint said he would like to meet such a person. Few were of such a nature as to garner praise from the local transportation suppliers!

"Oh, they're just very good people. Most of the Indios aren't, but when you get a good one, they're easily the best people in the world!" Julio replied.

Clint bit back a reply. That was better than the usual attitude of many of the Spanish toward the Indios. The blacks were always denigrating toward them, even when they had close family connections.

Clint went in to be introduced to Orlando Ruiz and family, who he knew very well. They chatted for a few minutes and told Clint they had a deal with the one operating the mine that would allow them to do things for the community, which was part of the Indio culture. They had little personal ownership, and were responsible for the rest of their community, simply because they were part of it. That is what a man's reason to exist was about. That was an enormous difference in other cultures that most couldn't see. The Indios are part of a community, not someone who lives in a community.

Clint had made the arrangements with a big mobster, Paulo Lariez, who ran the mine for these people. He was now accepted and part of that community. That gave him a real sense of pride.

The next drive was on out the road and over almost to Costa Rica, then return to Puerto Armuelles. He didn't see anything more that got his interest, though he looked at two properties the taxi driver said were for sale to stay in character.

They returned to the town a bit before dark. Clint made arrangements for the taxi to meet him the following morning to take him out another road, then went in, cleaned up, had a good meal at Yola's, bought a few small items from the vendors along the street, and went back to the brothel.

There were a lot of people at the place. Gina, a girl Clint knew, came to talk a bit and to offer her services, but Clint said, at his age, last night made it good for the week. He bought her a drink and chatted a few minutes. He said the girl the night before had said that some Russian came in a lot and that he wanted to treat the girls like slaves, so she didn't like him. Was that the one she was talking about? Ivan?

He pointed to a large, slightly loud, stocky man with longish dirty blonde hair and a moustache. He was smoking a cigar, which is against the law in Panamá inside a building where others were present. She made a sour face and said that was Ivan! She didn't like him, either – but he paid. Very well. He refused to abide by the rules. That cigar was enough to make her want to puke!

Clint grinned and stood. He went to Ivan, who was trying to pull a girl into his lap.

"Sir, take your hands off the lady – and put out that offensive cigar."

"*What*?! Who the *hell* do you think you are?"

"I am a customer who has made an objection to your manner and to that cigar. There is a law here that says you may not smoke inside a building occupied by other persons. Put it out and conduct yourself like a human being, not like a pig!"

"I'll wipe the floor with your stupid ass! You don't tell me what to do!"

"Anytime you feel you may survive such an attempt, feel free to make that attempt. Meanwhile, you will put out the cigar."

People were amused and nervous. This was some old man confronting a younger and much bigger man. Ivan jumped up and reached to grab Clint – and found a sword cane blade against his throat. "I'm quite capable of defending myself against riff-raff of your type. Sit down, put out the cigar, and keep your hands off the employees here."

He looked uncertain. Clint slightly increased the pressure on the blade, drawing a drop of blood.

Ivan sat. He put out the cigar. Clint sat opposite him and studied him.

"So. Now we understand one another. We may act as though we're civilized.

"I spent many years in Europe and in the field of protection of certain parts of the population. I met many of our type there. I learned how to act like I am also civilized. I managed to retain the better skills such occupation requires. I have had more confrontations than I care to remember where only one was able to walk away. I am still here.

"You are Czeck?"

"Siberia."

"Ah! A very cold and forbidding place. I was there only three ... four times. Some years ago. It is a hard life there."

Ivan cocked his head to the said. "I can't figure you at all! Who sent you? Taylor?"

"I know no Taylor. I am merely here on a small vacation

and am looking for a place to retire. I wish to establish a reputation, for the first time in my life, of being a good person to know and one who is sensitive to others. You are merely a convenient person to use in that pursuit. It isn't personal. I do feel I am, at last, gaining a bit of a more reasonable perspective on life. I find that I actually like some of the people here. I have never liked anyone before. It is a confusing and good feeling."

"You would have cut my throat if I'd come after you, wouldn't you?"

"A small flick of the wrist. All these people noted that you physically had attacked me when I simply asked you to abide by the laws here and put out that cigar. I even, another first time, have a permit for the cane as a personal defense weapon."

He nodded. "You want to move here?"

"I begin to believe that would be a good move."

"Looking for work?"

"I have more wealth than anyone reasonably needs. I think not, when I consider the lines of work at which I am adept."

He laughed. "I think I like you! No horseshit, just tell it like it is!

"Girl! Bring my friend a drink!

"I'm Ivan Gregor."

"Which is not your name, but possibly part is. I am called Generoso Morales here."

"Which is not your name, but possibly part is."

"It is what my present passport says."

"Yeah. My passport says that is my name, but reversed."

"What is your line of work, if you don't object to my asking?"

"I'm a mining engineer. We've found a lode of, uh, silver near here."

"Toward the north and west? A taxi took me there as a point of interest in an area where I might come to live."

"Yeah. Indio people live there. It's their farm where we found the silver mine. They're people I like. Good people. I don't think they like me too much. We're too different."

"Yes. I spoke with the family. They would make no judgements about you. If you haven't had much congress with them, they probably only have a very slight feeling, one way or the other."

The girl brought Clint a Scotch and soda (which he didn't like) and a vodka straight for Ivan. They chatted awhile. Clint learned, indirectly, that the uranium was very close to the silver, which he suspected.

He went back to the hotel to go on the wireless with his laptop. He wanted to learn something about the extraction of uranium.

The taxi was waiting. Clint took the driver to breakfast, saying he arose a bit later than usual. He was quite tired last night.

"Yeah! Not tired enough to keep from telling our local pain in the ass Russian where he gets off!" he replied. "I would liked to have been there!"

"Oh, he's a rather common type in Europe, in the worse areas. He watches too much telly and thinks he can make the world into that drivel. He merely needed it explained to him that people will tolerate only so much."

"Gina said he called you his friend and bought you expensive drinks. She thought you were the most gallant and macho person she ever saw! You stood up to a person everybody around here is scared of and made him back down!"

"Then she, also, watches too much of the telly silliness."

They were already semi-pals. This made him a real pal.

Later, while driving around the local countryside, Clint managed to learn that there was a second crusher area near the silver mine. Julio said there was one truck going out there a lot that the Russian was driving. He didn't like that. Foreigners weren't allowed to operate equipment as heavy as that truck in Panamá. He pointed out the little rutted road the truck went up. Clint acted like it was a little interesting, but said he didn't know anything about mining, and didn't want to.

They went out on a little peninsula where Clint already owned (thanks to Manny) some property. There was a large rocky plot for sale, but nobody seemed interested. It was the plot that caused Manny to buy his plot – to put an end to the big development planned on the plot after they could manage to buy the part Manny bought just before they made the deal. Bummer!

Clint went back to town about four. He figured he was able to piece a lot of it together. What he'd learned about uranium meant a tremendous amount of rock had to be crushed to get a small amount of uranium. Critical mass wasn't much, but he would have to crush and process quite a few tons of rock to get enough for a bomb.

Julio never saw anyone but Ivan going out that road. He was doing it himself. Clint wanted to know how he was managing it so that he could get away with the thing. He also wondered if that bunch had already gotten enough uranium out to make a bomb. That may have been what they were doing when this started. Wouldn't the automatic detectors find something like uranium?

Not if it was in thick lead containers. That would be heavy.

Clint didn't think they had done that. There was some-thing else they wanted him to be distracted from.

Not necessarily! They wanted to keep him on the Bocas

side so he wouldn't ever learn what this was about, and so that he'd never find the uranium mine. They knew he had set the silver mine up, and that he knew the family there. That meant the road to the uranium mine went into the back of the property. It was a very big place, and Orlando surely wouldn't know about it. He wouldn't allow it.

Clint decided he was going to go up that road to find out what they had and exactly how they were handling it.

Clint waited until dark, then went by El Critico to see if Ivan was there. He was.

Clint could trust Julio, so had the taxi take him to the road. Julio said he could take the taxi up that road, so went in. If anyone asked, there was no fence or gate on that road, so it was legal to go on it. There wasn't even a sign saying it was private.

The road went around a few small hills, then into Orlando's property for only a hundred fifty meters or so. There was the truck and a big pile of crushed rock just outside a shed. The crusher was inside the shed, which was insulated so that little sound would escape. There was a radiation suit on a rack. There were three lead containers, one open and empty, the other two sealed. From what Clint understood, the two containers would mass at about half critical mass, together, judging by the volume in each. If some was sent out it was probably a shipment of three containers to make up half the critical mass. All they would need was these three filled. Clint would see they didn't ever receive the last three. He told Julio to go outside, then he put on the radiation suit. He opened the two sealed containers and took the tubes of uranium out and told Julio to stay at least twenty feet from him as he took it into the hole the rock was taken from. He hid the tubes in a crevice about twenty feet into the hole, then went back to the shed to hang the suit where it was when he came in. He went back out and Julio took him back to town. He cleaned up and was at El Critico by ten o'clock, saying he had been detained by another Russian. Did Ivan know who he was? He looked much like Ivan, but was a little thinner and was darker.

Ivan said he didn't know anyone else there from Russia. Was Clint sure he was Russian?

Clint remembered the pictures of Niklev and Ghenkof from the net. He said he had assumed that, as the accent was the same. This one said his name was Viktor. He had a scar on his face and across his nose, but it was not bad. He made the description close enough to fit Ghenkof or Niklev. Neither had a scar on their face, but that was a common fixture in disguises.

That really made him nervous! "Did he have a gold tooth just to the side of the center?"

"I did not notice."

He talked for a minute, then mingled. Ivan soon sneaked to the door and out. Clint waited, then went out himself and to the hotel to grab some sleep. About four in the morning Ivan knocked on his door and asked if the Russian he met was carrying anything, or were there packages he was watching.

"No, I don't think so, but there could possibly been something in the car waiting for him."

"There was a car? There was someone in the car?"

"Yes. A woman, I think. I found it odd when she didn't come out to be introduced. She stayed in the car.

"Of course, it may not have been his car. She may have been waiting for someone else."

"There were some things stolen from my place. They're terribly dangerous. They are poisons you have to understand to use. I'm afraid someone might have taken them and could let them get in the water or something. That would be a disaster! I must find them!

"I wish I knew who took them. I'll be in terrible trouble if someone, er, misuses them. It wasn't quite legal for me to have them, you see. If someone is harmed or killed by them I could be in serious trouble."

"Well, I hope you find something like that and neutralize it! Those kinds of things should not be carelessly left around! It alarms me one as professional as you seemed to be would allow any chance of such an occurrence at all!

"I think I understand! You had them in a safe place, but someone specific would take them. True? Someone who will use them for personal reasons that are not to the good of anyone else?"

"Much too close to the truth."

Clint said he wouldn't know anything about that kind of people here. He was here to escape that life and those kinds of people.

Ivan soon left. Clint got a little sleep and met with Julio and Orlando. He got Orlando aside and explained the situation, and that he was Clint Faraday. Orlando said he was suspicious of this strange Spaniard and could not help feeling he already knew him. They would see nothing else was ever moved from that property. Orlando suggested that he could take a few random people to see his property and could accidentally find the shed and mine. He would then, as it was not legally on his property, put guards on it to see that it was closed and abandoned. Clint said it might even be a good idea to have someone there with a Geiger counter who was looking for radium in that kind of place. They might avoid going into the mine.

Orlando said he knew just the person to set that up!

Clint had introduced Orlando to the mobster, now ex-mobster, who opened the mine. Paulo Lariez. He had no doubt Orlando and he had become friends and confidants. He would arrange it as someone from his mine who came from Mexico to look for anything he could find in the area.

"Ivan's luck sucks lately," Clint remarked. They all laughed.

Clint felt this part was fairly well arranged, so went back to the hotel. Ivan came in about four and said he had made no progress in finding the poisons and he couldn't find but one person, a taxi driver, who had seen the other Russian. He spent most of the day looking for that person.

It suddenly dawned on him that the poisons are easy to detect, so it was possible they were still hidden at his place. He would go back and check. Maybe he'd see Generoso at El Critico later. With a proposition, if it was truly the people he suspected who stole the poison.

Clint said he would quite possibly be there.

He hung around the pier awhile, greeting the locals he knew. None saw through his disguise.

He cleaned up and went to El Critico at seven for dinner. The food was good there. Ivan came in about seven thirty, excited and scared. He said some people were on his property and had as much as thrown him off! They had all his things!

"Call the police, as much as the idea annoys us who have been in the occupations we have been in."

"I can't. It's not really my property. I thought we had an agreement with the owner, but it turns out my, er, associates didn't bother with that little detail. I'm in terrible trouble!"

"Well, you can at least disclaim any knowledge of the stolen poisons. That should, as the yanks say, get you off the hook for that."

"Not really, but that's not the ... my problem will be with others, now. A war between two different groups will end with one of them wiped from the face of the Earth.

"You see, the stolen poisons were the factor that gave the group I work for precedence in, er, some areas. Now they're no longer a factor. If the other group learns of that, well, it can get bad. Fast!"

"Distance yourself from both sides. If you were merely working as a contract worker for one side you are no part of the management, shall we say."

"I wish I could. I suppose I'm a walking dead man, but that's part of the trade. I do think I like you. Don't get involved with Russian groups. They play for keeps. It's always a survivors' club deal."

Clint nodded. "Take care," he said. "I really have to leave tomorrow for a few days. Three days. It's to renew the visa."

"You bother with that crap?"

"I wish to retire here. I wish for a solid good reputation. Yes, I bother with it."

"Oh, that's right. I guess it's better. I suppose I'll be gone, one way or another, before you get back. I wish you good fortune and hope you can retire the way you want."

Clint thanked him and said he hoped it could be resolved where he wouldn't end up dead. He went to the hotel.

He left for David in the morning. Paulo Lariez called to say the little problem with the illegal mining operation was settled. Orlando made a deal with a US company about the uranium and was now several million dollars richer – which he hated! They would go together and build a new school in the town where Orlando's wife grew up. And a free medical clinic.

Clint could picture Orlando's response to the news that he was a few million dollars richer. His reaction the first time was, "What the hell will I do with it?"

Clint caught the early bus to David in the morning.

"Clint? What's happening down there?" Judi demanded. She called just after he got on the bus.

"What have you heard?"

"That some spies were doing something and some

Spanish guy came in and broke it up."

"Not quite. I'll tell you about it when I get back."

"Nando is back."

"Oh? That's news! It might work out pretty well, all-in-all."

"He and Serg seem to have come to a Mexican standoff of some kind. I wondered if maybe you engineered that."

"No. I haven't heard from Sergio. He might have figured I'd like for Nando to be where I can see him."

They chatted, then Clint called Manny, who said he had some fairly complete reports about part of it, but not so much what it was about. He knew a very important mine was closed down.

"The missiles?"

"Uh-huh. It was a wild scheme that could have ended up with a lot of people hurt, but in the old Soviet block."

"Clint! Do *not* get involved with those people! They're crazy!"

"So Ivan said. I was involved, like it or not."

"I'm glad to hear that you *were* involved. No more?"

"Not really. They get in worse trouble if they come after me than they do if they cut their loses. They'll be too busy trying to survive than to worry about me. I think, from what I learned, that two weeks and it would have gotten really hairy for some people."

"I see. They would have been able to convert a missile in two more weeks?"

"If I've figured the process right, about that."

"It's stopped?"

Clint thought, then answered, "I think they'll all be looking for a way out. Nando is back in Bocas Town. I think I can defuse another piece of it through him. Those people are crazy. They're not stupid."

They talked a little more. It broke up the boredom of yet

another three hour bus ride.

Clint decided not to stay in David. He got off the bus and went to the Hotel Porto del Sol to become Clint Faraday again, then caught the bus for Bocas. It was an uneventful trip, though Clint got a bit of a feeling of deja vu when they passed the Rambala Road. He talked with several people in Chiriqui Grande, then went on to Almirante and home. Judi greeted him and came over with coffee, but he said what he wanted was a couple of Balboas, then a little rest, then a meeting with Nando – after getting updated by Sergio.

Not a lot was on his comp. He cleaned up the whole thing, then went to the police station to chat with Sergio. Things were maintaining a sort of nervous peace. He asked about the yacht that had been there for several days (That kind of stuff is handled by the police, checking visas and so forth) and was told they were a bunch of French and Belgium tourists who had left, then gone to Chiriqui Grande for two days, then were sailing for Europe.

That set off bells! "Stop that boat! Get Interpol and the coast guard and anyone else you can in on it! I have to call, a friend," Clint cried.

"What's on that boat?" Sergio asked, looking shocked.

"Nuclear fuel."

"Shit! For real?" Sergio seldom used anything any stronger than "Maldicion!" (Literally, "Bad Word!")

"I think so. We may be able to stop this before it gets out of hand."

He went into the front room and called a friend who was an undercover agent for Interpol. He quickly explained what he knew and what he suspected. Manolo said they couldn't do anything until the yacht came into a national area, but he would have it watched every inch of the way to be sure they didn't transfer anything to anybody. It could be done through the satellites.

Clint went back in and talked a bit more with Sergio. He suggested that he would talk with Nando, then might want him held for ID check or something. Sergio said they could hold him on a very solid charge of suspicion of homicide. Clint agreed that was fairly well set, so long as it wasn't a direct charge. He *was* suspected.

He went into town and to the Laguna, where Nando was staying. Nando was sitting on the porch, and called to Clint as he approached. Clint went to sit across from him.

There was a short silence, then Nando said, "How much do you know?"

"All of it, now, I think."

Nando smiled. "I don't think you have a hint of what it's about. It's not what you think."

"Nuclears. Two factions who want control of an area. Bad news if either gets the top hand for everyone in the area."

He looked surprised. "We were warned to keep you out of it."

"The bit with the rednecks. You or them?"

"Them, if it matters. They acted on the word of a person who was reporting to both sides. He has disappeared. It was stupid beyond belief that they involved the Indios.

"Tell me, would you have even cared if that wasn't done?"

"I wouldn't have asked anymore about it. If something else brought it up I would've gone after it."

"I wonder if they got enough of the product out to accomplish more than threats."

"They haven't yet delivered it to the European connection. It won't arrive."

That was even more of a shocker, it appeared. Nando stared at him a moment without speaking. He was suddenly sweating.

"Your dodge with the yacht was as stupid as the other distractions meant to head me off."

"I see."

"You're, as Frandrev said about his own case, a walking dead man, aren't you?"

He looked like he was about to cry. "I have to get out!"

"As Gregor also said, it's part of the trade. You knew that from the start."

"You have to help me! They'll kill me!"

"What? You hire yourself out as a killer, then want to cry when it's your turn? It's what you signed up for. There isn't a way out."

Nando was staring at the table top when Clint got up and walked out. Sergio was in front of the China. Clint waved and shook his head. If Sergio arrested him now and held him it would be his responsibility when he was killed. Clint had learned to be pragmatic where these kinds of people were concerned. If they were lucky, Nando would leave and never arrive somewhere else.

Now it was time to wait again. Clint didn't believe for one second this was over. They would try the same stunt somewhere else if they weren't stopped here and now.

"Clint, you've started a firestorm. It's lucky it won't be here, to any extent," Manny reported. "Would you believe those cruds tried to get my old organization to help them?

"I mean, Ruskies? We'd have anything to do with them – particularly when what they wanted was for us to hit some others who were helping them? Gimme a break!"

"I think we have a little more to go," Clint warned. "Don't let out the least hint you know anything at all about it, other than I went all over hell an...!"

"What?"

"I just thought of something I said on the comarca fifty or a hundred years ago, or so it seems, when I got drawn into this.

"I'll be damned!"

"What?"

"I told some people I'd see them in hell."

"The rednecks?"

"Uh-huh. Some things just clicked."

"They're gone. I kept a close eye on them. They're exactly what they appeared to be."

"Exactly! They're what they appeared to be."

There was a pause, then, "Don't do that."

"Oh. They appeared to be inordinately stupid gringo rednecks."

"And that's what they are."

"Another something to stop me from finding the real source of the problem."

"Two factions from the old Soviet Union who were trying to grab control over each other. That ain't it?"

"Oh, I suppose it was, at least in their own minds."

"It's better if I don't know what the hell you're talking

about?"

"It's safer for your family. Those people are capable of anything."

He could picture Manny looking thoughtful and nodding. They chatted a minute or two more, then Clint rang off. He would wait until the yacht was stopped and the uranium seized before making a phone call.

What to do in the meantime?

He got his boat and he, Ben, Earl, and Judi went fishing.

"Hi, Clint!" Fredrico, a friend from Almirante, called from his boat as he was passing. Clint had gone to the Lemon Grass with Judi, Ben, and Earl for dinner the night before. Clint met a girl from Australia and they spent the night together. Clint was laying in the hammock on his deck with coffee. Anita had gone with friends to take a tour of the islands and to snorkel off the Crawl Key end of Bastimentos. He returned the greeting.

Judi had finished watering her orchids and had called that she was going into Bocas Town for a meeting of the community watch group. Ben and Earl came by and knocked on the door. Clint called to "Come in!" and they came out onto the dock. Earl grinned at Clint and Ben said he should wear clothes when he was around. He drove him crazy.

"You and Earl serious?" Clint asked.

"Semi. It could work. He's wild and fantastic in bed, but he has to go back to his job in Phoenix next week. We just stopped to say hi and to tell Judi that Nando sneaked out last night."

"She's at the community center."

"We know. We saw her when we were leaving. I just wanted to show Earl what I have to put up with. You dress – or don't dress – like that and keep turning me down."

"Not my bag."

"Nobody says that anymore."

"I do!"

The computer dinged that he had a message. He sighed and went in. He usually didn't bother, but he was waiting for a message.

Done. M. Rpt fndg ltr.

Manolo. They'd stopped the yacht. He'd let Clint know what they found as soon as he knew.

Clint thought, then decided to wait. He wanted all the facts when he made the phone call.

"Important?" Ben asked when he went back out to his deck.

"Yes and no. It's what I expected."

"Want to go out in your boat? I'd like to show Earl a few of the islands close. Maybe I can convince him to move here and make me settle down."

"I have to wait for a couple more things. You can take the boat. It's right there. The keys are on the peg."

"I knew you'd do that! I'll fill it."

Clint nodded. Ben went back to his place to get their bathing suits and gear. Clint chatted with Earl. When Ben was gone, he said, "Is it serious with Ben, or are you just to distract me?"

"It's gotten serious. I am gay, and Ben is one hell of a nice guy, as well as as good a lover as I've ever known. I also love this place. The people are the best."

"You job's terminated, you know."

"No, I didn't know. I had my last report late yesterday. I suspected things had caved."

"They stopped the yacht."

He nodded. "I'm not in deep enough to be in any real trouble. Let them think I've got you fooled?"

"If you're honest with Ben about the emotional thing, no

problem. Don't ever mess with my friends or involve them in this kind of crap."

"I've learned enough that I take that as a very strong and honest warning. I think I like Ben too much, but it either will or won't happen. I swear he won't be in any danger."

Clint nodded. Ben came back in, carrying the stuff. Earl said Ben was right. He couldn't seduce Clint either. They were laughing as they got into the boat.

Clint dressed as much as he ever did in Bocas Town and went to chat with people at the Golden Grill, then to go to the Rosa Blanca for some farmacia needs, then to the China, then back home about eleven thirty to deep fry some breaded shrimp and French fries. Except the French fries were yuca. He hung around for about two hours, fixing this and that around the place before the comp dinged.

2/3 M CM. Done.

They found the uranium. They had 2/3 enough to make a bomb.

The comp dinged again. *Turn on your phone.*

Clint checked the cell phone. It was totally discharged, so he plugged in the charger and called Manolo.

"Just wanted to fill you in. There was some resistance, and the regular people couldn't go aboard. They were followed and a small boat came alongside. Some men came out on deck with AK-47's and threatened them. The last thing they learned in life was that you don't threaten people with automatic weapons if they have them too and don't wait for you to make the first move. They then boarded, there was some shooting, then they went back to their boat and left. They waved for the, er, police officials to go on aboard. They found the stuff and a few other things.

"So! How are things in, as you were overheard to say,

Glock-amora?"

"Say something intelligent and it fades away before the words are out. Say something stupid and it's there for the rest of your life," Clint replied. "Where did the little boat come from?"

"We don't know. They did us a favor and we won't ask."

They chatted awhile, then Clint decided to make his call. He hesitated before he punched the number, then called Manny instead.

"You have anything to do with a bit of a shootout in the Atlantic a couple of hours ago?"

"It was five and a half hours ago and to what doest thou refer thus and thusly?"

"Thanks from about six governments around the world. Did you ever learn anything about any of the others involved in this crap?"

"Not really. They're very adept at hiding their trails."

Clint told him they found the stuff. He knew it. They talked a minute, then Clint made the call. To Armakov.

"Hi! Surprised Eladio didn't answer! How are things?"

There was a silence.

"You there?"

"Clint. What, I mean, you caught me off guard. People seldom do. You are a very surprising man, it would seem."

"You had to know I'd figure that out. I just want to know what the real motive is. Or was."

"To stop them. I told you that."

"Good enough! Now the rest of it."

"To get my hands on the uranium. You seem to have prevented that."

"Nobody needs that kind of thing."

"It would only be for our protection."

"At first, maybe. In a few more months or years someone would want to do to others as others almost did to them, and it would be the same thing, just another one at the top. You know it."

"There wasn't yet enough to make the device. That is the thing that would not be explained."

"But the threat, not the actual device, was the power play."

Armokov sighed. "I have worried about that. Perhaps it is better if things remain the way they are, bad as they are. It would probably only get worse."

"I'm afraid it will, anyhow. That's ingrained in the psychology of the area, and no one's trying to change that."

He sighed again. "True. Sad, but true."

"It's over. Stop the psychology here. That will be a start."

"But time is extremely limited. You don't know the plans many have. There are those in Panamá as well who plot and plan. There are those in Brazil and Ghana and Egypt and Germany and England and Australia and any other place you care to name. I fear civilization as we know it is very near to extinction."

"I agree. I don't care to be part of that."

"You, as an Indio, can go into the jungle and escape the horrors to come. We, in the cities of the world cannot. It is something we, as a race, do to ourselves."

"That's the thing none of you will actually accept. You say it as rhetoric, that's all. You do it to yourselves."

Armakov sighed again. "That is true. Hasta lluego." He hung up.

Clint sipped the coffee and took a bite of the hojaldre, then waved at Judi. She waved back and called that she had some news. He said he'd be over later.

After taking care of the things around his house he checked over the boat. He would go out later, anyhow, so put his gear in the boat and went to Judi's deck dock. She told him that Nando was supposed to go straight to Changuinola, had left Almirante, and no one had seen or heard a word from him since.

Clint wondered if he had enough savvy to be able to disappear himself, or if others had caused the disappearance. As stated several times, he knew the rules when he got in the game. To sit around crying about it when it didn't go your way was to sit around and cry about it when you'd lost. There was one way out of that, and that was to die. Clint held no sympathy for the type.

Earl came by to say he and Ben had a sort of promissory deal. He would go back to the states and would quit his job, take care of some unfinished business, then move here. If things worked out the way they seemed headed he would be a permanent fixture around the place. He swore again that Ben wouldn't ever be in any danger.

"I have some things to guarantee they'll leave me alone. I'm not important enough to be in deep. It'll be better to let me out than to face what can happen. It's because of family. I'm in it at all because my father was. They were the only ones I was ever around until I got a job and worked with other people. I didn't even know there were good people in the world before that. I didn't know I was gay, either. I thought everybody felt the things I felt. They just never acted on it and never talked about it because they'd be ostracized if they did. It took a guy where I worked to show me the reality of the world.

"Anyhow, I'm really happy here. Nobody cares if I'm gay or straight or bi.

"I might be bi. Ben is, if not much. We dated girls twice, and I really did have a good time, and I really did like the sex, it just isn't the kind of thing I like best. No girl makes me go weak in the knees, and Ben and a couple of others had that effect on me.

"What I'm saying is that Ben and I will be a couple. Maybe not exclusive, but maybe."

"I wish you all the luck in the world," Clint replied. "Ben's a good person. A lot of people here are. I think you'll fit."

They chatted, then Earl went back to Ben's. Clint called Manny, who didn't have anything new and hoped he never did about that bunch. If they never came up again in any way it would be fine with him. Dave called and said he was going up the coast. Did Clint want to go?

No. Clint wanted to stay right there for at least a week. No headaches and no buses or boats.

Manolo called and reported both bunches of the nuclear deal were neutralized and wouldn't ever have a chance to do anything like it again. He had no doubt they'd try.

"Just so they leave my friends and me out of it," Clint replied. "If there's a next time, the last thing they want to do is get me or any other Ngobe involved." Manolo said he'd heard Clint was declared a Ngobe. Congratulations! It was an honor few ever knew. Sergio called and said they found a body that might be Nando in the swamp on the flatlands. He had the ID papers of Nando on him, but the body was in bad shape. They would identify it as Nando, but this one was about three and a half inches shorter than Nando. Too bad they didn't have any of his DNA.

"Let it lay unless it turns out to be someone who was just there when he needed a body," Clint suggested. "If it's someone from around here who was caught up in it through no fault of their own, make it loud and clear it wasn't him. Those people will make sure the next one *is* him!"

He then went to the Golden Grill to talk with people, then did a little grocery shopping for vegetables, then went home.

His phone buzzed. It was shown from a private number.

Clint shrugged and answered. It was Armakov.

"Clint? Just wanted to let you know. There was a minor revolution in a certain country that replaced a few of the more important leaders who had delusions of grandeur. The information that initiated it was things that they had hidden so deeply they thought it would never be found.

"You?"

"No. I'm through with anything to do with those."

"Well, if you know who did it, tell them thanks from ninety percent of the people in at least three countries." He hung up. Clint wondered. Manny?

No way! Manny wouldn't get involved in that kind of thing. He wanted out of that crap, and was staying out of it very well here. He called Manolo and bluntly asked him if his organization was behind it.

"They would be the ones with that kind of information, so I imagine a few of the groups got together and solved the problem for a few months or years. They have special operatives for that kind of thing. You can bet what happened here had a big something to do with it. Nuclears? No way will that be forgotten or forgiven!"

"Well, Armakov said to tell whoever did it thanks from ninety percent of the people in at least three countries."

"They did it to themselves. They tried to use you. Bad

move!"

"I didn't have anything to do with it."

"You exposed it. That was the same thing. Those people can thank you."

"Crap!" Clint retorted, with feeling.

C. D. Moulton's works are available on most major outlets as printed or e-books. CD writes the CD Grimes, PI mysteries, the Det. Lt. Nick Storie mysteries, the Clint Faraday mysteries, the Flight of the Maita science fiction series, books on orchid culture and many others of many types. Mystery, adventure, intrigue, science fiction, fantasy, para-normal, mild erotica, and factual.